THE Charles Dickens

CHILDREN'S COLLECTION

Published by Sweet Cherry Publishing Limited
Unit 36, Vulcan House,
Vulcan Road,
Leicester, LE5 3EF
United Kingdom

First published in the UK in 2020
2020 edition

2 4 6 8 10 9 7 5

ISBN: 978-1-78226-483-5

Charles Dickens: The Old Curiosity Shop

Based on the original story from Charles Dickens,
adapted by Philip Gooden.

Cover design by Pipi Sposito and Margot Reverdiau Illustrations
by Santiago Calle, Shading by Luis Suarez
from Liberum Donum Studios

www.sweetcherrypublishing.com

Printed and bound in China
C.WM004

Charles Dickens

THE OLD CURIOSITY SHOP

Sweet Cherry

LIFE AT THE OLD CURIOSITY SHOP

Our story starts with Nell
Trent. Nell's parents
died when she was
very young. She was
thirteen years old
now and could barely
remember them at all.

Nell lived with her
grandfather. He was
kind and caring,
and best of all,

he ran the strangest and most mysterious shop you could ever imagine. The Old Curiosity Shop sold everything from ancient suits of armour and rusty swords to antique chairs and tapestries.

Nell and her grandfather lived in the little flat above the shop. Their lives were full of fun and magic. In the winter, Nell would read to her grandfather by the fireside. She told him stories of heroes and dragons

and knights. Her grandfather, in return, told her stories of her mother, and how Nell looked and spoke just like her. In the summer, they often walked in the fields and played hide-and-seek among the green trees. They came home tired but happy.

Nell's grandfather employed a young man called Christopher Nubbles to work in the shop. Everyone called him Kit. Kit looked younger than he was, with a cheery, boyish face that was forever stretched into a smile. He was very fond of Nell and always tried to look out for her.

Nell's grandfather wanted to do the best he could for his granddaughter. He knew that he wouldn't live forever, and he worried about what would happen to Nell after he was gone. The Old Curiosity Shop did not make much money, and so Nell might be left in poverty.

Yet, strangely, people believed that
the old man was rich. They thought
the simple life he and Nell led was all
pretend – a way to hide their riches.
One person who believed this was
a young man called
Richard Swiveller.

Truly, Richard was
a kind-hearted fellow,
but he was not very
smart and was rather
lazy. It crossed his
mind that it would be
a good idea, one day,
to marry Nell Trent.

After all, if Nell's grandfather was rich, then Nell would inherit lots of his money when he died. Then she would share it with Richard.

What Richard did not know, however, was that there was no money at all. They had so little money, in fact, that Nell's grandfather turned to gambling. He would spend hours playing card games, trying to win a fortune for his dear Nell. But the more games he played, the more money he lost. He never won a single penny, let alone a fortune.

Desperate, Nell's grandfather decided to borrow money so that he could keep on gambling. That's when the trouble really started.

He borrowed money from a man called Daniel Quilp. Quilp had an office on the river bank, opposite the

Tower of London. He lent money to people, which they had to pay back with extra on top. If they couldn't pay back the money then he would take away whatever property or possessions they owned.

Quilp was *not* a pleasant person to meet, or even to look at. He was very short, but his head was large enough to fit the body of a giant. He had mean black eyes and wiry black hairs sprouting from his chin. His fingernails were crooked and long.

But Quilp's worst feature by far was his smile. When he pulled back his lips, it revealed the few hideous, yellow teeth that were left in his mouth. Even Quilp's voice was horrible. It was sharp and cutting and had no trace of kindness at all.

'Your last loan was seventy pounds,' Quilp spat at Nell's grandfather. 'You lost it all in one night and could not pay me back. Why would I lend you more money?'

'It will be different this time, Mr Quilp,' answered the old man. 'I have dreamt three nights running of winning a large sum.'

'Oh, you have had a *dream*, have you?' sneered Quilp. His mouth hung open in that rotten smile.

'Please!' pleaded the old man. 'Don't help me for my sake, help me for the sake of Nell.'

'Nell? Oh yes, the orphan,' said Quilp. 'Poor little Nell.'

'Everything I have done has been for her,' said her grandfather.

Quilp drew out his pocket watch and made a show of examining it very carefully.

'I'm sorry, I can't stay,' he said, not sounding sorry at all. 'I have a business meeting.'

Of course, Quilp did not *really* have a business meeting. As he walked out

of The Old Curiosity Shop, Quilp looked back and saw the sadness on the grandfather's face. He smiled.

Quilp liked nothing more than making people unhappy.

THE ESCAPE

After realising that Quilp would not
lend him any more money, Nell's
grandfather thought that everything
was lost. His sadness soon turned
to illness and before long he became
very sick.

Nell looked after the old man as best she could. But things only got worse.

Quilp took possession of their flat and of The Old Curiosity Shop. 'If you had just paid me back the money,' Quilp said, sneering, 'then I wouldn't have had to take this hideous shop from you.'

Quilp told his lawyer to write a few legal documents to prove that the shop should be his. The lawyer, Sampson Brass, was a thin, weasel-like man with a voice that always managed to sound both bored

and scared at the same time. He did everything Quilp told him to.

Sampson Brass was also Richard Swiveller's boss. Richard used to hear Sampson blabbering on about Nell and her grandfather and The Old Curiosity Shop. Sampson was another person who believed that they were hiding their riches, which is why Richard believed it too. But when Richard heard that Nell and her grandfather had lost their shop and home, he felt sorry for them.

One of the first things Daniel Quilp did when he took over The Old Curiosity Shop was fire Kit Nubbles. Kit was unhappy about this, but there was nothing he could do.

Daniel Quilp and Sampson Brass moved into the rooms behind The Old Curiosity Shop. They didn't actually want to live there. They just wanted to make life uncomfortable for Nell and her grandfather, who were still staying in the flat upstairs – for the moment, at least.

Quilp smoked furiously on his pipe. It was as if he were trying to smoke out the ill old man who lay in the upstairs bedroom.

Nell's grandfather recovered a little but not fully. For Quilp, this was enough. Quilp came to see him one evening. The old man was sitting in his chair, and Nell sat on a stool beside him.

'I'm glad to see you well again, at last,' said Quilp, sitting down opposite them. 'You're quite strong now?'

'Um, yes,' said the old man, feebly.

'Good,' said Quilp. 'Because you can't stay here much longer.'

'I suppose not,' said Nell's grandfather.

'I have sold the things.'

'Things?' asked the old man. He was confused, but Nell knew exactly what Quilp meant.

'The furniture, the swords, the dusty old tapestries – all that rubbish you kept in your shop,' said Quilp. 'Now, when shall it all be moved out? Hmm … shall we say this afternoon? You can leave at the same time.'

'This afternoon! Can it not wait until Friday?' answered the old man.

Quilp sighed. 'Very well, but no later.'

Thursday evening came and Nell's grandfather seemed more like himself. He asked Nell to forgive him for having lost their shop.

'Don't talk like that,' said Nell. 'There is nothing to forgive.'

'Well, we will not wait here to see all the furniture taken away and the shop emptied out,' said the old man. He said they should leave early the next morning before Daniel Quilp or Sampson Brass were awake.

'We will travel on foot through the fields and woods, and by the side of rivers,' he said. 'Anything is better than staying in this shop that was once ours and is now *his*.'

He could not bear to say Quilp's name.

At sunrise the next morning, the two crept downstairs. They paused every time the stairs creaked, worried that they would wake

Quilp and Sampson. But they did not need to worry. Terrible snoring was coming from the back room, where the men were sleeping. They sounded like two pigs competing to make the most noise.

Nell and her grandfather reached the front door and eased back the rusty bolts. Fresh, cool air greeted them. It was a beautiful early morning in June. The sky was deep blue, without a single cloud.

Nell and her grandfather were
free from Quilp. Free, but poor.
Where would they go next?
How would they live?

NELL'S LONGEST ADVENTURE

Nell and her grandfather had endless adventures on their journey across the country. It felt as if they were living in one of the stories Nell used to read.

They travelled with a couple of men who roamed the country putting on puppet shows. Then they met

a woman who trundled waxwork
figures in a wagon from town to
town. Everywhere she went, she put
on an exhibition.

Nell did little bits of work as they travelled, for small amounts of money. She repaired the ragged puppet costumes and gave out leaflets advertising the travelling waxworks exhibition. Sometimes her grandfather helped in these little tasks, too. Nell watched over him anxiously. It was as if he were the child and she were the grown-up.

For the most part Nell was happy, but she still had nightmares. Every night she dreamt of the large, grinning face of Daniel Quilp. Sometimes, she even thought she glimpsed his mean black eyes and hideous smile in the streets they passed through.

༄‿༄

After trudging through busy towns and tiny villages, Nell and her grandfather were glad to reach the

open countryside. Nell loved the countryside. She loved looking at the green, rolling hills, and breathing in the fresh, crisp air.

But neither the green grass nor the fresh air changed the fact that they were often cold, hungry

and tired. They depended on the kindness of people they met for food and shelter.

At last, their luck changed. They met a schoolmaster called Mr Marton. He was a simple, modest man.

'I'm heading to a village not far from here,' Mr Marton explained, as the three of them stood on the green hills at the border of England and Wales. 'I am going to be the new teacher in the village school. Why don't you join me? I'm sure we can find you somewhere to stay.'

At first, Nell and her grandfather were unsure. But when they looked into each other's cold, hungry faces, they knew they had to go.

In the small country village there was an ancient church, with green ivy growing up its walls. Near to the church sat a pair of old stone houses.

One of these houses was to be the schoolmaster's. The other was

empty. The hundred-year-old man who had been living there had sadly, but rather unsurprisingly, died. His job had been to look after the keys of the church, to open and close it on Sundays, and to show it to visitors.

Mr Marton went to speak to the vicar, who was an old friend of his. He told the vicar all about Nell and her grandfather.

The kind vicar quickly agreed that Nell and her grandfather should be given somewhere to stay. So they moved into the empty stone house,

and Nell became the new caretaker for the church.

'I know it's not perfect,' the vicar said to Nell. 'An old church is a dull and gloomy place for someone so young. I'm sure that you would rather be out dancing or playing or running about the fields than taking care of a dusty old building.'

'I do not mind,' Nell replied. Truthfully, she was glad to have found such a peaceful, sheltered spot for her and her grandfather. She worked hard to make the little stone house comfortable for them both.

She repaired the tattered curtains and carpets. Mr Marton trimmed the grass and the overgrown plants

outside. And her old grandfather helped both of them where he could. It wasn't long before the little house began to look like home.

Nell and her grandfather quickly found friends in the village too. Everything was right again – or so it seemed. But the weeks of travelling across England, often cold, tired and hungry, had not been good for Nell's health. She became paler and weaker by the day. She often caught her grandfather looking at her, his face crinkled in worry.

BACK IN LONDON

Kit Nubbles had been miserable since Nell and her grandfather left London. He had not only lost his job at The Old Curiosity Shop, he had lost his friends too. But, before long, Kit found a new job with a family called the Garlands. There was old Mr and Mrs Garland

and their grown-up son, Abel
Garland. They were a happy family,
who lived in a thatched cottage on the
edge of London.

Kit was given a room above their
stables and asked to look after their
horse.

Everything about the place was perfectly neat and tidy and nice. Even the other servant in the household, a young girl called Barbara, was neat and tidy and nice. And pretty, Kit noticed.

Kit Nubbles might have been happy again, but Daniel Quilp was not. He was angry because Nell and her grandfather had slipped out of The Old Curiosity shop on that fine June morning without him knowing about it.

It wasn't that he wanted to say goodbye to them. Well, not in a friendly way, at least. He'd been looking forward to personally pushing them out the door of their old home. To sneering at them as they ambled down the street, tears

in their eyes. He would have stood on the doorstep nodding his large head and rubbing his hands together with glee at the sight. But they had got away. He had missed a chance to make someone miserable and he could not stand it!

So it was very bad luck that one day, when Quilp was in the worst mood he had been in all week, he spotted Kit.

Kit often returned to The Old Curiosity Shop. He liked to look in the windows and remember the amazing things that once filled them.

On the day that Quilp saw him, he had even brought Barbara with him, to show her where he used to work. Quilp was watching from the dusty downstairs window of The Old Curiosity Shop. He was so short that he only just reached over the windowsill; so short that Kit and Barbara did not see him there.

Quilp did not know who Barbara was. To him she was just a girl – a servant judging by her clothes. But he could see that every time Barbara smiled, Kit smiled too. 'Disgusting,' Quilp muttered under his breath.

He simply *hated* to see people smile.
Quilp decided there and then to wipe
the smile off Kit's face.

He found out that Kit was living and working with the Garland family. Then he had a word with Sampson Brass, his lawyer. Strangely enough, Sampson was also the lawyer for Mr Garland. That meant that Sampson and Mr Garland often sent each other letters. Quilp suddenly had a very clever, very evil idea. 'Make sure,' he told Sampson, 'that any letters from Mr Garland to you are hand-delivered. Tell him you will only receive his letters if he gets Kit to deliver them personally.' Sampson nodded and a cruel smile stretched across Quilp's face. 'And when Kit brings a letter to your office,' he whispered, 'here's what you'll do next ...'

THE PLOT AGAINST KIT

You probably remember that Richard Swiveller worked at Sampson Brass's office. One day, the two men were talking. The lawyer said that he had recently lost several small sums of money – or rather that they might have been stolen.

As he was speaking, Sampson held up a five-pound note and examined it against the light. Then he slipped the note into his desk, hidden among some papers.

Richard Swiveller was confused by this. 'Um, sir,' he said. 'You seem to have put your money in your desk. You should put it back in your pocket or you might lose it.'

Sampson chuckled. 'Oh no. Not now. I'm going to leave it there,' he said. 'After all, I know *you* are not a thief. I have complete trust in *you.*'

Then he sent Richard off to deliver some papers to another lawyer nearby.

Next, Kit Nubbles arrived with a letter from Mr Garland. Sampson welcomed him.

'Take off your hat, Kit,' he said. 'Make yourself at home.'

Sampson took Kit's hat and placed it on the desk. It was a large,

battered old hat. Sampson moved
the hat around two or three times.
Then he shuffled the papers on
his desk, as if he were looking for
something. Then, strangely, he told
Kit that he had to leave the room for
a few minutes.

Sampson came back at exactly
the same moment Richard Swiveller
returned from running his errand,
and he asked Kit to leave. As soon as
the door shut behind Kit, Sampson
flew to his desk and rummaged
through his papers. 'It's gone!' he
shouted. 'Gone!'

Sampson looked in his desk and under it and on it. Then he slapped all his pockets, one after another.

'That rascal Kit has taken my money,' he said to Richard. 'Run after him!'

The two men ran out of the office. Kit had not gone far. They soon caught up with him.

'Stop!' cried Sampson, laying his hand on one of Kit's shoulders.

Richard Swiveller grabbed the other shoulder. 'Not so fast, sir. We need a word with you.'

They took him back to Sampson
Brass's office. Kit was confused,
then frightened. His face drained
of colour and turned a sickly grey.
But Kit knew that he was innocent.
'Search me,' he said, pointing to his
clothes.

Sampson snatched Kit's hat and handed it to Richard. He himself rummaged in the pockets of Kit's coat. He fished out a few small items, but there was no money at all.

'Check inside his hat,' Sampson snapped at Richard.

Richard drew out a handkerchief that was tucked inside the lining of the hat. Then he gasped. There, nestled within the handkerchief, was the missing five-pound note.

Kit was stunned.

Richard Swiveller was surprised too. He never thought that Kit might be a thief.

Sampson Brass *pretended* to be surprised. But, of course, he wasn't really. It was he who had slipped the five-pound note inside Kit's hat earlier. And it was he who had made sure that Richard discovered the 'stolen' money.

A police officer was summoned and poor Kit was taken away.

Things went from bad to worse for Kit. He spent long days and longer nights in prison before being put on trial for robbery. His case was heard at the most famous court in London, the Old Bailey.

The judge boomed at him: 'How do you plead? Guilty or not guilty?' 'Not guilty,' Kit answered in a trembling voice.

Sampson Brass was a witness against him. Richard Swiveller was a witness against him too, though he did not want to be.

There seemed to be no explanation as to how the five-pound note had got inside Kit's hat. No explanation except that he had put it there himself – that he had stolen it.

The jury whispered and sniggered and sneered, and eventually said that Kit Nubbles was guilty. He was to be banished from London and sent to Australia as his punishment.

The news of Kit's fate hit Mr and Mrs Garland and Barbara like a lightning bolt. They were not prepared to lose their servant and their friend. Richard Swiveller was upset too. He was so upset, in fact, that he fell ill.

THE END OF
DANIEL QUILP

It turned out that Sampson Brass's
maid had overheard the lawyer
plotting with Daniel Quilp. She had
heard Quilp telling Sampson to plant
the five-pound note on Kit and then
pretend that it had been stolen.

She had kept the secret to herself,
because she was frightened of
Sampson Brass. And she was even
more frightened of Daniel Quilp.
But she could not stay quiet any

longer. Now that Kit was about to be sent to Australia, the maid knew what she had to do. She told Richard Swiveller everything she had heard.

Richard was delighted. Kit could be saved! Richard's illness suddenly vanished. He hopped straight out of bed and ran to tell the Garlands. The Garlands then went to see Sampson Brass.

Old Mr Garland was very angry. His face was cherry red and he scrunched his wrinkled hands into solid white fists.

Sampson shook his head and stuttered, 'But – but, it was not *my* fault. It was all Mr Quilp's idea.' Then the cowardly lawyer wrote out a confession and signed it.

⁓⁓

Night was drawing in. Daniel Quilp
was sitting in his office near the river.
He was furious. His plan to get Kit
Nubbles into trouble had gone badly
wrong. Now it was he who was in
trouble. Serious trouble.

There was a loud knock on the
front door.

'Open up!' boomed a deep voice.
Knock. Knock. Knock. Heavy fists
slammed against the door. 'Open up!
It's the police!'

But Daniel Quilp was as sneaky
as he was cruel. He slipped out of
the back door and slid into a dark
alleyway.

The night had settled in and a mist
had risen from the river, making it
impossible to see anything. Quilp
stumbled along, hands outstretched
to feel his way.

From behind him came more
shouts.

He stumbled forwards, lost his balance … and fell.

Suddenly he was submerged. Cold, dark water filled his mouth and his

nose. He splashed desperately, but
the current was too strong. He took
a deep breath and tried to swim, but
a dark shadow loomed over him.

He reached out his hand and felt something smooth and slimy. It was the hull of a huge ship; a ship that pushed him further and further

under the water, until he disappeared into the inky depths. Daniel Quilp was never seen again.

The
End of Nell

Unfortunately, not all endings are happy endings, and this one is not very happy at all.

Of course, Kit Nubbles was delighted to be freed from jail. And the Garlands, Barbara and Richard Swiveller were delighted to have their friend back. But Kit's happiness did not last long. One morning, just as the sun was peeping through his bedroom window, he received a letter from Mr Marton, the schoolmaster who lived next door to Nell and her grandfather. The letter said that Nell was very ill and that Kit should hurry to see her.

Kit told Mr and Mrs Garland and Barbara and Richard. Together they travelled to the country village where Nell and her grandfather lived.

By the time they reached the small stone houses, winter had arrived. Tiny, crystal-like snowflakes had begun to fall. They covered the grass in a sparkling white carpet.

Kit burst through the door of Nell's little house and ran to her bedside. 'Nell!' he cried. 'Nell, I'm here.'

But he was too late. Nell had breathed her last breath.

Her poor grandfather cried for days. Within a few weeks, he too passed away.

But Nell left behind happy memories in the minds of others, especially the schoolmaster, Mr Marton, and the children in the village. And in the mind of Kit Nubbles, of course. Kit never stopped thinking about his old friend and the times they had shared together in The Old Curiosity Shop.

Not long after Nell's death, Kit married Barbara. Then he shared his memories with her, and with their children. Kit sometimes took them to the street where Nell had lived. But it was not the same. The Old Curiosity Shop had been pulled

down long ago and replaced with a wide road.

At first Kit would draw a square on the ground with his stick, to show his children where the shop used to stand. But he soon became uncertain of the spot. Was it here, or over there?

Time swept the bricks and stone away. But it could not brush away the memories. In the minds of Kit and his family, Nell and her grandfather lived on.

Charles Dickens

Charles Dickens was born in Portsmouth in 1812. Like many of the characters he wrote about, his family were poor and his childhood was difficult. As an adult, he became known around the world for his books. He is remembered as one of the most important writers of his time.